READ!

These levels are meant only as guides;
you and your child can best choose a book that's right.

UP TO 50 WORDS

Level 1: Kindergarten–Grade 1 . . . Ages 4–6
- word bank to highlight new words
- consistent placement of text to promote readability
- easy words and phrases
- simple sentences build to make simple stories
- art and design help new readers decode text

UP TO 100 WORDS

Level 2: Grade 1 . . . Ages 6–7
- word bank to highlight new words
- rhyming texts introduced
- more difficult words, but vocabulary is still limited
- longer sentences and longer stories
- designed for easy readability

UP TO 200 WORDS

Level 3: Grade 2 . . . Ages 7–8
- richer vocabulary of up to 200 different words
- varied sentence structure
- high-interest stories with longer plots
- designed to promote independent reading

MORE THAN 300 WORDS

Level 4: Grades 3 and up . . . Ages 8 and up
- richer vocabulary of more than 300 different words
- short chapters, multiple stories, or poems
- more complex plots for the newly independent reader
- emphasis on reading for meaning

LEVEL 2

Library of Congress Cataloging-in-Publication Data Available

2 4 6 8 10 9 7 5 3

Published by Sterling Publishing Co., Inc.
387 Park Avenue South, New York, NY 10016
Text © 2007 by Harriet Ziefert Inc.
Illustrations © 2007 by Elliot Kreloff
Distributed in Canada by Sterling Publishing
c/o Canadian Manda Group, 165 Dufferin Street,
Toronto, Ontario, Canada M6K 3H6
Distributed in the United Kingdom by GMC Distribution Services,
Castle Place, 166 High Street, Lewes, East Sussex, England BN7 1XU
Distributed in Australia by Capricorn Link (Australia) Pty. Ltd.
P.O. Box 704, Windsor, NSW 2756, Australia

I'm Going To Read is a trademark of Sterling Publishing Co., Inc.

Printed in China

Sterling ISBN-13: 978-1-4027-4243-9
ISBN-10: 1-4027-4243-6

For information about custom editions, special sales, premium and
corporate purchases, please contact Sterling Special Sales
Department at 800-805-5489 or specialsales@sterlingpub.com.

I'm Going To READ!™

TIC and TAC
CLEAN UP

Pictures by Elliot Kreloff

Sterling Publishing Co., Inc.
New York

"Our house is dirty," said Tac.
"Let's clean it up."

"Okay," said Tic.
"Let's clean."

Tic and Tac cleaned the bedroom.

the   was   cleaned

The bedroom was so clean!

Tic and Tac cleaned
the bathtub.

The bathtub was so clean!

Tic and Tac washed
the dishes.

The dishes were so clean!

Tic and Tac cleaned the porch.

The porch was so clean!

I'M TIRED!

Tic said, "I'm tired of making
everything so clean!"

windows   I   floor   then

"If *you* wash the windows
and I scrub the floor, then . . .

everything will be clean!"

"Now I'm hungry!" said Tic.
"I want to eat."

"But you can't get
the dishes dirty," said Tac.
"I just cleaned them!"

"So I'll take a bath,"
said Tic.

"But you can't get
the tub dirty," said Tac.
"I just cleaned it!"

"So I'll take a nap,"
said Tic.

TAC

TIC

No!
No!

"No! No!" yelled Tac.
"I just made the bed!"

Tic asked, "So what *can* I do?"

"You can go outside," said Tac.

"You can take a shower."

"You can take a nap."